「親愛的寶貝，今天是你的生日，祝你生日快樂☺」
"My dear boy, today is your birthday. Happy birthday to you!"

哇！你好可愛啊！

Wow! How adorable you are!

我是 Cloudy！汪汪！
I am Cloudy! Woof-woof!

嘿！生日快樂！快過來
送你一個小禮物

Hey boy, happy birthday! Come here.
This gift is for you!

今天是你生日呀！
Hey! Today is your birthday!

早安，生日快樂！
Good morning dear. Happy birthday!

歡迎壽星一起來玩！不要忘記喔！
Come and have fun together, birthday boy! Don't forget it!

Cloudy, 好像就在那邊

Cloudy, it seems to be over there!

生日快樂！
生日快樂！
壽星優先唷

Happy birthday!
Happy birthday!
Birthday boy first!

嘻嘻！
我們今天好幸運呀！
Hee! We are so lucky today!

你看！那邊好像很好玩耶！
Look! It looks like fun over there!

好羨慕他們都有
爸爸媽媽陪著一起玩
I'm so envious
that their mom and dad are with them!

還有我啊！汪汪汪！
I'm here for you! Woof-woof!

生日快樂！我們一起玩好不好！
Happy birthday! Let's have fun together, shall we?

生日快樂!
讓我們來為你唱一首生日快樂歌吧!
Happy birthday! Let us sing a birthday song for you!

今天好開心唷！
大家都祝我生日快樂！
I'm so happy today! Everybody wishes me a happy birthday!

你看這個！
Look at this!

跟你說呦
媽媽每天都會放一顆蘋果在我的書包裡
我最喜歡蘋果了！你也喜歡嗎？

Tell you a secret.
Mom puts an apple in my schoolbag every day.
I like apples most. Do you also like apples?

哇～地上這些是什麼呀？
Wow! What are these on the ground?

聽說花園裡的花朵
會收集大家的願望

I heard the flowers in the garden
collected people's dream.

真的嗎?
Oh！Really?

你看！
他的願望是想要成為一個畫家耶！
Look! His dream is to be an artist!

那你的願望是什麼？

What about your dream?

我們再去那邊玩～走吧！走吧！
Let us have some fun over there! Go go!

你看！你看！水底下有星星耶！
Look! There are stars under water!

許個願望吧！
Make a wish!

我願望許好了，那你呢？
I've made a wish! How about you?

♪ ♪ ♫ ♩
早安！生日快樂！
祝你生日快樂，祝你生日快樂……
Good morning!
Happy birthday to you! Happy birthday to you...

Mr. Cloudy

世許我們都有一個夢
那個夢
曾陪著我們一起　很久很久很久

這本創作特別獻給我的愛犬
A-PUN（2004 – 2016）
說好的，再和我一起完成未來的夢想
打勾勾。

Maybe we all have a dream that has been with us for a long long time.

This special book is dedicated to my beloved doggy, A-Pun (2004-2016).
Make a pinky promise. Let's chase our dream together again.

生日快樂 HAPPY Birthday

作者│林彥良・阿蕉 BaNAna Lin 選書企劃│黃昱禎 美術設計│黃祺芸 社長│張淑貞 總編輯│許貝羚 行銷企劃│洪雅珊

發行人│何飛鵬 事業群總經理│李淑霞 出版│城邦文化事業股份有限公司 麥浩斯出版 ADD │ 104 台北市民生東路二段 141 號 8 樓
TEL │ 02-2500-7578 FAX │ 02-2500-1915 購書專線│ 0800-020-299 發行│英屬蓋曼群島商家庭傳媒股份有限公司城邦分公司
客服專線│ 0800-020-299 csc@cite.com.tw 劃撥帳號│ 19833516 戶名│英屬蓋曼群島商家庭傳媒股份有限公司城邦分公司

香港發行│城邦〈香港〉出版集團有限公司 ADD │香港灣仔駱克道 193 號東超商業中心 1 樓 TEL │ 852-2508-6231 hkcite@biznetvigator.com
馬新發行│城邦〈馬新〉出版集團 Cite(M) Sdn Bhd ADD │ 41, Jalan Radin Anum, Bandar Baru Sri Petaling, 57000 Kuala Lumpur, Malaysia. TEL │ 603-9057-8822
製版印刷│凱林印刷事業股份有限公司 總經銷│聯合發行股份有限公司 ADD │新北市新店區寶橋路 235 巷 6 弄 6 號 2 樓 TEL │ 02-2917-8022 FAX │ 02-2915-6275

ISBN │ 978-986-408-861-4 初版二刷│ 2023 年 1 月 定價│新台幣 480 元 / 港幣 160 元 Printed in Taiwan 著作權所有 翻印必究

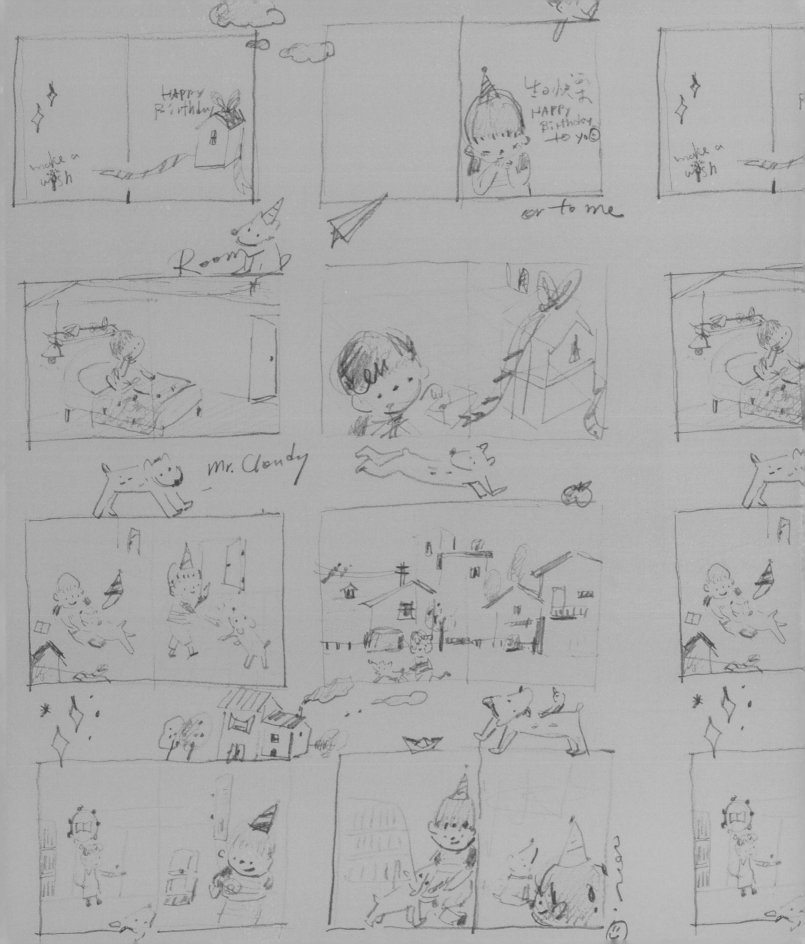

Garden

play Ground